For Scarlett from Mummy

First published in Great Britain 2009
by Egmont UK Limited, 239 Kensington High Street, London W8 6SA

Text and Illustrations copyright © Lydia Monks 2009

Lydia Monks has asserted her moral rights

ISBN 978 1 4052 3258 6 (Hardback) ISBN 978 1 4052 3259 3 (Paperback)

A CIP catalogue record for this title is available from the British Library

All rights reserved

Printed and bound in Malaysia

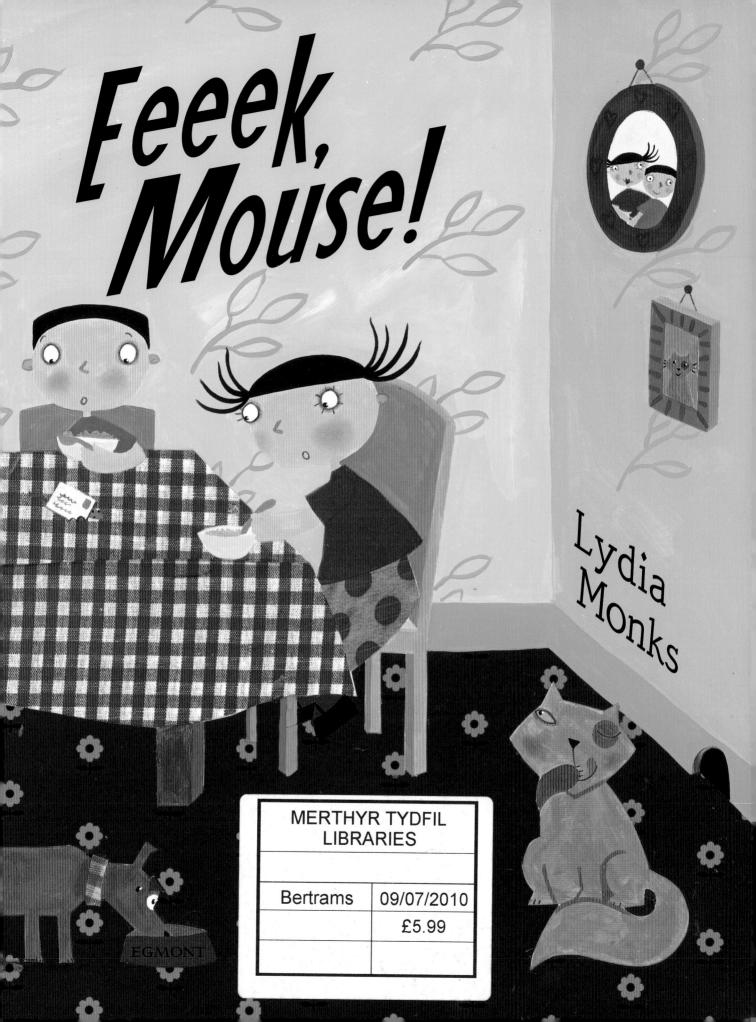

Eeeek, Mouse!

Lydia Monks

EGMONT

"**Eeeek**, a mouse!" squeaked Mummy one morning.

"Aaahh, I don't like mice!" squawked Daddy.

"This must be where it lives!"
said Minnie.

I hope so.

"How can you
not like mice?"
said Minnie.

I do!

"They are so cute,
with their really big ears,
and their twitchy noses
and their lovely long tails . . ."

"Mice nibble
anything
and everything,"
said Mummy.

"They give
me the
heebie-jeebies,"
said Daddy.

(* They make
a scrumptious
squeaky snack!)

"We must build a cunning trap," announced Daddy.

"Nooo, you can't do that!" said Minnie.

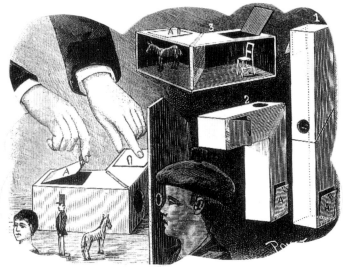

"Don't worry," said Daddy. "I won't hurt it. I will catch it, and let it go free in the countryside."

"But something might eat it," said Minnie.

But Daddy wasn't listening.
He had already started working
on his super-dooper trap.

Minnie ran to her room.
She had a cunning plan
of her own . . .

In the middle of the night, Minnie tied a piece of thread to Daddy's super-dooper trap.

The piece of thread was attached to a tiny little bell.
If a mouse fell into Daddy's trap
the tiny little bell would ring
and Minnie would hear it
and go and rescue the mouse.
The bell was so small that only she would hear it.

ting! ting!

Later that night, the bell gave a little tinkle.

Minnie tiptoed downstairs and peeped into Daddy's super-dooper trap. Peeping back at her was a teeny weeny little mouse.

Minnie whispered, "Hello, little mouse. I've come to rescue you."

Minnie picked up the mouse very gently, and took it up to her room, where she put it into its new mouse house which she had lovingly prepared.

The mouse seemed very pleased.

Daddy wasn't very pleased the next day when he discovered that his super-dooper trap wasn't so super-dooper after all.

"I haven't caught a thing," he said. He decided to make a few adjustments.

The next night,
to Minnie's surprise,
the little bell rang **again**.

ting! ting!

There was **another**
teeny weeny mouse
peeping up at her.

The same thing happened
the next night,

ting!   *ting!*

and the night
after that.

Minnie couldn't believe her luck.
She hadn't just saved one mouse,
she had saved
a whole family!

They all seemed very happy
in their new mouse house.

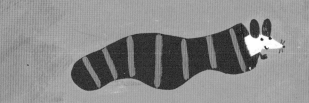

But none of them
had noticed the cat.
He had a
cunning plan
of his own.

This was the chance he had been waiting for.
He got closer and
closer and
closer until . . .

. . . he fell and landed
right on top of
Minnie's head!

"Run for it!"
shouted Minnie.

Eeeek!

Minnie had saved
the mice again!
But from now on,
she would have to
be more careful.

The next morning,
Daddy gave up on his
not so super-dooper trap.

"The mouse must have gone, or
else the cat caught it," said Daddy.

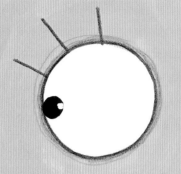

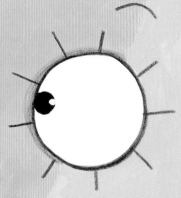

Minnie smiled.
"Yes, Daddy,"
she said.

"I think
the mouse
must have found
a nicer place
to live."

And so it had.
Minnie knew she
would have to keep
her squeaky secret safe.

She just hoped
the cat didn't
have any more
cunning plans . . .

ENJOY MORE BRILLIANT BOOKS

BY Lydia

No More EEE-Orrh!

Dicky Donkey drives everyone crazy!
Each morning they wake up to
EEE-Orrh! EEE-Orrh!
All the neighbours want to send him away,
until the day **Dicky Donkey** loses
his voice all together and is rushed to
the animal hospital.
Suddenly they miss him!

ISBN 978 1 4052 1740 8 (paperback)
ISBN 978 1 4052 2919 7 (board book)

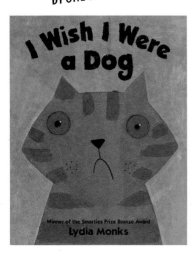

I Wish I Were a Dog

Kitty is fed up with being a cat.
Dogs have all the fun.
But then she finds out that maybe
being a cat isn't so bad after all.

ISBN 978 1 4052 1246 5 (paperback)
ISBN 978 1 4052 1751 4 (board book)
ISBN 978 1 4052 3438 2 (book and audio)

Aaaarrgghh, Spider!

All Spider wants is to belong
to a family. The trouble is,
she SCARES everyone too much!
Poor Spider. How will she ever
get people to like her?

ISBN 978 1 4052 1044 7 (paperback)
ISBN 978 1 4052 2319 5 (board book)
ISBN 978 1 4052 3044 5 (book and audio)

Mmmm, very tasty titles!

Ooo Ooo Ooo Gorilla!

Gorilla goes to stay with his friends.
They take him skating and skiing,
but Gorilla doesn't like it.
Then he discovers something
he **does** like doing, and
that's when the fun begins!

ISBN 978 1 4052 2754 4 (paperback)